CAROLINE SMAILES was born in Newcastle. In 2005 a chance remark on a daytime chat show caused Caroline to reconsider her life. She enrolled on an MA in Creative Writing and began writing.

If Caroline could choose a super power she would rather like a combination of teleportation, time manipulation and feet that are roller-skates. The reasons why, she feels, are obvious.

Caroline lives in the North West of England with her husband and three children. She can be found at www.carolinesmailes.co.uk and on Twitter as @Caroline_S

NIK PERRING lives in Cheshire, UK, where he writes, mostly, short stories. The stories he's written have been widely published, in the UK and abroad, in print and on-line. They've been collected in the book *Not So Perfect* (Roast Books, 2010), read at events, printed on fliers and used, with one of Dave Eggers', as essential material on a creative writing course in the US.

If Nik could choose a super power he would rather like the ability to type a little faster. Either that or be able to talk to cats. He likes cats.

His online home is here: nikperring.com and he's on Twitter as @nikperring

DARREN CRASKE began his career writing and illustrating comic books before his published work with book one of the Cornelius Quaint Chronicles: *The Equivoque Principle*. The second book in the series, *The Eleventh Plague* followed soon after, with the conclusion to the series to be published in 2012. Darren lives in Hampshire with his wife and two children.

If Darren had a super power it would be to define once and for all whether trees falling in a forest make a sound even if no one is there to hear it.

Darren can be found online at his blog http://theargonauts almanac.blogspot.com and on Twitter as @DarrenCraske

ALSO BY CAROLINE SMAILES
Disraeli Avenue
In Search of Adam
Black Boxes
Like Bees to Honey
99 Reasons Why (eBook)

ALSO BY NIK PERRING
Not so Perfect

ALSO BY DARREN CRASKE
The Equivoque Principle
The Eleventh Plague

CAROLINE SMAILES
AND NIK PERRING

Freaks!

Illustrated by Darren Craske

The Friday Project
An imprint of HarperCollins*Publishers*
77–85 Fulham Palace Road
Hammersmith, London W6 8JB

www.harpercollins.co.uk

First published in Great Britain by The Friday Project in 2012

1

A catalogue record for this book is
available from the British Library

ISBN 978-0-00-744289-8

Typeset in Minion by G&M Designs Limited,
Raunds Northamptonshire
Printed and bound in Great Britain by
Clays Ltd, St Ives plc

To all who, if only for a moment,
felt that they didn't belong.

'*But Lord! to see the absurd nature of Englishmen, that cannot forbear laughing and jeering at everything that looks strange*'

SAMUEL PEPYS (1633–1703)

THE FREAKS:

Some of these stories have been written by Nik. Some of these stories have been written by Caroline. Some we've written together. But in the true spirit of superheroes, we couldn't possibly reveal our identities.

THE STORIES:

The Photocopier. Statuesque. Charlie and the Bees. The Six Days of Stetson. She Sees Too. The Freak Show. Clipped Wings. In Her Basket. Fifty Per Cent (1). Fifty Per Cent (2). Invisible. Sixteen. Faulty Baby. Dancing With Annie. Soup. The Boner. Hello. One Day. Zombie Bangers. Getting the Girl. They Are There to Listen. Weight. Molly. Dear You. Control. No Sudden Movements. Dream Lover (1). Dream Lover (2). Once I Caught a Fish Alive. Before I Lost You. The Plastic Boy. Translated. The Girl Who Made People Glad. My Boss. My Lover's Shoes Don't Fit Me (Any More). Skinny Bitch. The Watermelon King. Dolly's Magic Sweater. Jimmy Swift. Damaged. My Dad's Boyfriend. Betty. I Want You to Ride Me Like a Pony. Magic Beans. Boy. What He Said. Wish You Were Here (1). Wish You Were Here (2). Beauty. Maman, Flying.

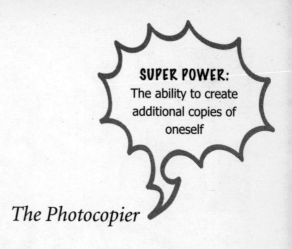

SUPER POWER:
The ability to create
additional copies of
oneself

The Photocopier

The day after me thirteenth birthday me mum said she had something massive to tell me. At first I reckoned she was going to say that me dad wasn't me dad or that she was pregnant with Bill from next door's sperm, but instead she just stood up and started spinning on the spot. At first I reckoned she'd lost the plot but then she started exploding.

CLIPP!

POW!

ZOWIE!

KRUNCH!

PLOP!

And five other mums shot out of her.

I swear to Christ it was the freakiest thing I've ever seen. There was me with wee in me knickers, with six of me mums standing there smiling at me like nutters. Me Main Mum said that the reason she was showing me her true self was 'cause she reckoned that I was a photocopier like her and that we'd know for sure in a couple of months.

I reckon I spent most of that year spinning on the spot in the front room with me six mums cheering me on, and me Main Mum telling me to spin faster or that I wasn't trying me hardest or that I needed to want it more. Course I never went

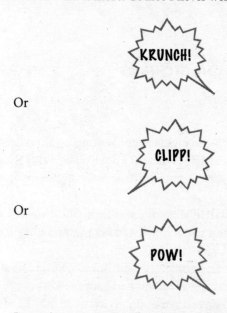

Or

Or

It was just me getting dizzy and trying not to throw up on me mums' carpet. But still, every day, I kept practising me spinning, faster and faster on that very same spot, hoping to Christ that one day me mums'd say I'd done good.

After that year me six mums sat me down and me Main Mum told me that they reckoned it was time I gave up me spinning. She said they'd been talking, her and me other mums, and that they'd figured that I'd never be like them. Me Main Mum said they reckoned that it was about time I concentrated on being ordinary.

SUPER POWER:
The ability to turn
oneself to stone

Statuesque

I remember when I first asked Hestia about her fingers. She'd been shy about it which surprised me. I mean it's not like she'd ever tried to hide them from anyone: her fingernails were stone – it was obvious.

She told me it had started when she was little. She'd wanted a hug from her dad and he'd said no, he'd told her to stop acting like a baby.

'I felt it in my fingers and inside,' she said. 'It was cold and hard. And when I woke up next morning, this had happened.'

She held out her fingers to me and I wrapped my hands around them. They were rough against my skin and they were cold too.

Hestia's ankles were stone as well. When she was eight she'd not been invited to her best friend's birthday party. She was so sad, she said, that she'd cried from the moment she'd walked out of the school gates to when she'd fallen asleep deep into the night. She told me that, the morning after, when she'd gone to pull her socks on, she'd found that her ankles were exactly the same as her finger-nails. Cold and rough and not really alive. She said she'd have cried if she'd had been able to, but she was dry.

4

To be honest I found her limp cute at the beginning, when we first met, when I told her it wasn't a problem, that we'd work something out. I think I have a thing for girls like that; in imperfection lies beauty, or something.

And I think that's why I like Amy. It's the braces and her lisp – I've always been a sucker for speech impediments.

She's a nice girl too. The best bit's her skin – I like how it's all smooth and warm and how she doesn't mind me touching it.

I guess I've got a problem, and that's what exactly to do about Hestia. I mean, I know I should tell her, but it's difficult. I worry about how she'll take it, about what it could do to her. You'd have thought that after eight years I'd know exactly how to handle her, how to handle this, but the truth is I've got no idea. I'm scared too. Recently her left breast became stone, completely without warning.

Maybe it's best to leave it, or maybe it's better to wait and see. Like I said to her all those years ago: we'll work something out.

SUPER POWER:
The ability to
converse with insects

Charlie and the Bees

Charlie liked to drink milk.
Three cups a day he would drink.

As an average.

The first would follow breakfast.

The second was taken from a carton with his packed lunch. And the third he would gulp down when he'd come home from school.

GULP!

He always gulped that one down in one **long** action.

Sometimes things **die**.

Sometimes things **fall**

and sometimes things **drown**.

There was a bee,

old and *tired*, and it fell into Charlie's after-school glass of milk.

It was hidden. And Charlie gulped the milk down in one *long* action.

The bee's legs and the bee's wings had come away from the bee's body and as Charlie gulped down the milk in one **long** action

the bee's legs and the bee's wings got caught between Charlie's teeth.

There were bees around the flowers, which were in bloom. The bees were not only

BUZZING

the bees were

CHATTERING

Sshhh.

Charlie said: 'Shh' and all the bees stopped,

and they rested on petals and leaves and branches and walls and windowsills and car bonnets.

After Charlie had finished his milk the next morning he stepped outside onto the pavement

and he began walking to the place from where he caught the school bus.

And Charlie heard what they said.

And the bees waited for Charlie to speak.

The Six Days of Stetson

The first time she wore that hat was on her hen night. She was eighteen then. 'You're too young for marrying,' her dad said to her. She'd only been seeing that one for a few weeks. 'I'm pregnant Dad,' she said. Her dad nodded because he understood. That night she took that pink Stetson out with her. She held it in one hand while she sipped lemonade through a stripy straw and watched all her mates having fun. 'Put your hat on,' some bloke said to her. She did. She put that Stetson on her head. That's when time stopped. That's the night that she snaked in and out of frozen people. Then she was tired and it was time for time to carry on.

The second time she wore that hat was when little Ruby was five months old. She wanted a bath. She wanted the screams to stop. She wanted her breasts to not be so leaky. That afternoon she put little Ruby on the bathroom floor and she climbed into that white bath. 'Put your hat on,' she said to herself. She did. And time stopped. That's the afternoon where she got to lie in a bath till her hands looked like her dead granny's. Then she missed little Ruby's noise and it was time for time to carry on.

The third time was at her dad's funeral. It was packed full of other people's grief. She took her hat along because it was a secret between her and her dad. It was sitting next to her on the pew. People saw that hat, pointed and smiled at it. 'Did William give you that?' a bloke asked. 'Yes,' she said. 'Put the hat on,' some woman said. She did. She wore it for her dad. And time stopped. That's when she sat for hours, maybe days, wishing that she could talk

with her dad for one last time. His dying had been sudden. 'If I'd known you were ill, Dad,' she said, 'I could have changed time.' Then she felt hungry and it was time for time to carry on.

The fourth time she was in bed with her husband. 'Let's try for another Ruby,' he said to her. She didn't want another Ruby. That's when she suggested the pink Stetson and her high heels. 'You kinky cow,' her husband said to her. She smiled. 'Put the hat on,' her husband said to her. She did. And time stopped. That's when she climbed off her husband's erection and went to take those pills that he didn't know about. That's when she sat on the bed for days and days, making sure that those pills were in her blood. Then she needed to be satisfied and it was time for time to carry on.

The fifth time was on the day Ruby started school. She wasn't ready for that change. 'I'll miss you today,' she said to Ruby. Ruby smiled and twirled around in her brand new school uniform. 'Shall I wear my pink hat to take you to school?' she asked Ruby. 'Yes Mummy,' Ruby said. She did. And time stopped. That's when she pulled Ruby to her and held her stiff little body as close as she could. She savoured every minute. Days passed. Then she missed Ruby's warmth and it was time for time to carry on.

Then there was that last time. That time when she was lying in bed with him. Her husband thought she was out with her mates, another hen night that needed her pink Stetson. She wasn't. That night she was lying naked in his bed. She was twenty-four then. She was old enough to know that she was in love for the first time. 'I love you,' she said to him. 'I know,' he said to her. That's when she realised that his eyes weren't looking like they usually looked. That's when he told her. He said, 'This can't go on.' She didn't speak. 'I've met someone who doesn't have a kid,' he said to her. 'She's not you but she'll do,' he said to her. 'It's easier,' he said to her. That's when she reached for her pink Stetson, when she pulled it from his bedroom floor. 'Put your hat on,' he said to her. She did. She put that hat on.

And time stopped.

11

SUPER POWER:
The ability to read minds and to hear the thoughts of others

She Sees, Too

I am in the doctor's surgery again.

The woman opposite is holding a dog-eared magazine about celebrities. But she is not thinking about the celebrities, she is not even reading it. No, she is thinking, worrying, about the man who's sitting to her right. She has looped her bag strap over her arm, to protect it. He intimidates her. It's his head, it's because it's shaven and it's because he's so thin. She thinks he's a junkie. Thinks that he needs to steal.

He, Shaven-head, is not thinking about stealing or about the woman. He is thinking about his cancer. He is thinking about his wife, and his children, and he is desperately trying to not cry. He is terrified and he is lost. He is drowning. He is playing a hopeful song in his head, drumming his fingers to its beat. He might survive.

A few chairs along sits a girl. So pretty and too thin. She hurts herself, starves herself. It makes her feel better. It is the only thing that makes her feel better – it *works*. And if her mother wasn't outside, waiting for her in the car, then she wouldn't be here at all. Her appointment will be a waste of time. She knows what she'll tell the doctor. She's a clever one, her. I like her. I smile.

She sees.
And she smiles back.
This is unexpected and for a moment I am stunned.

She looks away quickly. Too surprised to be embarrassed. She's worried that I'm thinking she's ugly, but I'm not. I like her. And she likes me – at least, she thinks she might. She doesn't know. She's scared. Confused. Feels fat.

I hear her turning it over in her mind. I can hear the static, the storm, the thunder of her worry.

'If he smiles at me again,' she says to herself, in her head, 'then maybe I'll stop. Maybe I'll change. Maybe this person's good. Maybe this is who I've waited for. Maybe this is who I need. Maybe. Maybe. I'm so scared.'

I hear the static in her brain.

'I will look at him,' she says, and even in her head her voice is shaky and weak. 'I will be brave. I will take a risk. I will be strong. I need this. I want something. Maybe this could be good. I am so scared.'

I can feel her head spinning. I can feel her fear; it's making a fist in my stomach.

She prepares herself.

Counts down. Starts at ten, then nine, then eight. She's so scared.

Of course, I know when she'll look, and I know what I have to do when she does.

So I ready myself. But I'm scared as well. I didn't expect this.

I want to smile back. I want to smile at her.

I don't want to let her down. This could be the start of something.

Be brave, I tell myself as she counts four, then three, then two. Be brave.

SUPER POWER:
The ability to look
beyond appearances

The Freak Show

'One woman's freak show is another woman's portrayal of courageous triumph over difficulty.'

ROLL UP.
ROLL UP!
COME,
COME TO THE FREAK SHOW,
THE GREATEST SHOW ON EARTH:
THE PLACE WHERE *LAUGHTER* IS *QUEEN!*
A SHOW OF *ODDITIES*,
A SHOW OF *ANOMALIES*,
A SHOW FULL OF SIGHTS
THAT WILL MAKE YOU *SQUEAL*.
MY FRIENDS,
STEP,
RIGHT THIS WAY.
LET'S MINGLE
WITH THE *FREAKS!*
HURRY,
HURRY,
HURRY,
MOCK THE LUCKLESS
ON DISPLAY.
ONLY
THE DEVIL TO PAY,
IF YOU STEP,
RIGHT THIS WAY.

COME!
MEET THE DISORDER CURIOSITIES
ONE, TWO AND THREE.
WE HAVE A *THIN* ONE,
A *FAT* ONE,
AND A SELF-HARMING GRAND ONE.
LOOK HOW HER *SCARS* GLISTEN
UNDER THE LIMELIGHT!
SUCH PLEASURES
WILL
ASTOUND YOU,
SUCH PLEASURES
WILL
ENCHANT YOU.
HERE, IT IS ALL FUN,
FUN,
FUN!

LISTEN!
WHAT'S THAT?
A VOICE THAT'S PURE?
A VOICE THAT'S TRUE!
WEEP
AT HER BRAVERY,
WEEP
FOR THAT FACE!
A FACE FOR RADIO,
A FACE SO *DREADFUL*.
AND *PORTLY* SHE IS TOO.
ROLL UP,
ROLL UP.
COME ONE,
COME ALL,
TO THE FREAK SHOW,
THE GREATEST SHOW ON EARTH:
THE PLACE WHERE *LAUGHTER* IS *QUEEN!*

OBSERVE!
SHE LOOKS LIKE YOU,
DOESN'T SHE?
BUT THIS ONE LIVES ON *HAPPY* JUICE.
LOOK, SEE!
HER *LOSS*,
IS OUR ASTONISHING *GAIN*.
JUG,
AFTER FLASK
AFTER *BOTTLE*.
AND FOR THE FINALE,
WHEN SHE VOMITS,
IT IS *SPECTACULAR*,
IT'S A GAGGING EXHIBITION
OF *PAIN*.
HURRY,
HURRY.
STEP,
RIGHT THIS WAY.

17

TEP,

RIGHT THIS WAY.
STARE,
AT THE *PLASTIC* PEOPLE!
A SAMPLE
OF THE MARVELLOUS *MUTANTS*
IN SHOW.
LOOK!
AT THEIR LIPS,
AT THEIR BREASTS,
AT THEIR NOSES.
ENVY THEIR
CRAFTED PERFECTION.
PEEK!
AT THEIR *SCARS*
SIGNED
WITH THEIR SURGEON'S *GLEE*.
A STICK
WILL
BE PROVIDED
FOR YOU
TO *PROD*
AND *POKE*.
ALL OF THIS YOURS
FOR AN UTTERLY TRIVIAL FEE.
SNIGGERING IS OPTIONAL,
WE *APPLAUD* WHEN YOU DO.
BE QUICK!
DISCOVER
THE UNABRIDGED SHOW,
NOW,
IF YOU HURRY,
HURRY,
HURRY.
ROLL UP,
ROLL UP.

LOOK, THIS ONE

APPEARS SOMEWHAT COMMON.
YOU'D NEVER SUSPECT
SHE'S A *RARITY*,
YOU'LL SEE.
OH YES,
SHE'S A WANNABE *FREAK*,
A STAR-STRUCK *FREAK*,
A RATTLING *FREAK* THAT WALKS
ON HER KNEES.
SEE!
HOW SHE FALLS
THROUGH THOSE CRACKS.
LOOK!
HOW HER EYES
ARE HOLLOW.
LISTEN!
HOW SHE WHISPERS
HIS NAME.
AN UNSOLVABLE PUZZLE
OF WHO TO BLAME.
LOOK AWAY QUICK,
BEFORE YOU CARE,
AS YOU
ROLL UP,
ROLL UP!
COME,
COME TO THE FREAK SHOW,
THE GREATEST SHOW ON EARTH:
THE PLACE WHERE *LAUGHTER* IS *QUEEN!*

STEP,
RIGHT THIS WAY.
COME!
WIND-UP THE LADY WITHOUT
HER ARMS,
WITHOUT HER LEGS.
WEIRD LOOKING CREATURE,
ISN'T SHE MAJESTIC?
I'M SURE YOU'LL AGREE!
SOME SAY SHE'S THE MOST
RIDICULOUS SIGHT
YOU'LL EVER SEE!
GO ON,
YES,
PLEASURE YOURSELF
BY ASKING.
WE KNOW WHAT
THAT THOUGHT
WILL BE.
HER SQUIRMING
WILL
FEED
YOUR FETISH,
IF YOU'RE QUICK.
IF YOU HURRY,
HURRY.
HURRY.

COME,
COME TO THE FREAK SHOW.
BE SURE TO HOLD YOUR BREATH,
DON'T DARE TO WHISPER A WORD.
RAGE!
ARISE
THE *ANGRY* WOMAN.
LOOK!
HOW SHE JIGS *UP*
AND *DOWN*
AND AROUND
AND *AROUND*.
LOOK!
HOW SHE'S JOURNEYING
NOWHERE
MAKING *OBSCENE*
SOUNDS.
LOOK!
HOW SHE BRANDISHES HER *FIST*
UP
TO THE HEAVENS.
WATCH!
HER HIDE FROM RESPONSIBILITY.
WATCH!
HER PARTY TRICK OF BLAME.
ACTION!
LET'S *SCREAM*,
LET'S RUN AWAY,
BUT
OH
WHAT *FUN*
WE OFFER TO *YOU*
TODAY.
ROLL UP,
ROLL UP.
COME,
COME TO THE FREAK SHOW,
THE GREATEST SHOW ON EARTH:
THE PLACE WHERE *LAUGHTER* IS *QUEEN*!

19

LOOK,
THERE'S THE ONE
WITH THE CREDIT
CARD.
ANOTHER SAMPLE OF THE JOYS
WE HAVE
IN STORE.
LOOK!
AT THE LINES OF WORRY
CARVED
INTO HER BROW.
WATCH!
AS SHE SPENDS,
SPENDS
SPENDS,
TO HIDE HER *PAIN*.
SHE LACKS BUT SHAME.
MONEY,
MONEY *MONEY*.
IT'S ONLY MONEY.
IF YOU'VE A SILVER COIN,
THEN WE'VE A SPECTACLE THAT
WILL
DELIGHT!
THAT WILL
ENTHRAL!
STEP,
RIGHT THIS WAY,
MY FRIENDS,
YOU CAN'T
GO HOME
WITHOUT
AN *EVERLASTING* SOUVENIR.
A LOST LIMB CAN LIMP,
PILLS CAN BE POP
POP
POPPED.
A RAZOR BLADE
WILL
EXCITE,
TOO MANY DELICIOUS POSSIBILITIES
WITHIN YOUR SIGHT.

BUT AT LAST,
IT'S TIME
FOR YOU
TO DECIDE.
SO STEP,
RIGHT THIS WAY.
COME INSIDE!
WITH YOUR SHINY SILVER COIN,
WITH YOUR *JABBING* STICK,
WITH YOUR PAPER BAG
FOR YOUR *SICK*.
MIRROR, MIRROR, ON THE WALL,
YOU ARE THE FAIREST OF THEM ALL.
OH DO,
OH DO!
COME,
COME TO THE FREAK SHOW,
THE GREATEST SHOW ON EARTH:
THE PLACE WHERE *LAUGHTER* IS *QUEEN!*

Clipped Wings

I met her on a Saturday. Saturday the fifth of February 1994.

I was ill, too ill. They thought I'd be a danger to myself and so they locked me up in a place that was full of freaks. That's where I met her, Sarah, she'd been locked up too.

I met her on my first night. 'You look normal,' she said.

'Thanks,' I said and we both laughed.

'What you in for?' she asked.

'Stuff,' I said and we both laughed again, because it was okay not to want to spill out your guts and it was okay to be fed up with talking.

Turns out Sarah wasn't like me, she was happy to talk. She said it made her feel better talking 'bout it, said that the more she talked 'bout it the less likely it was to disappear. I liked that. It made sense.

That first night, Sarah explained how the doctors and nurses had got it wrong 'bout her, 'bout how she wasn't suicidal, not even slightly. Sarah told me that she liked to fly, told me how she liked the feeling of falling with her arms outstretched, how she liked to fly to the floor. Sarah'd laughed, said the doctors thought she was depressed, manic, schizophrenic, suicidal, not quite right, said they'd wanted to clip her wings and make her normal.

'I just like flying,' Sarah said. 'It's what I was born to do.'

Over that first week, Sarah and me'd sit talking for hours. She told me all 'bout the places where she'd flown from, the ladders, the walls, the garages, the buildings. She told me 'bout how she was finding landing a bit of a bugger.

'I keep forgetting my feet,' she said.

She told me 'bout all the times she'd ended up in A&E and all the times that no one'd listened when she'd tried to explain that it was the landing and not the flying that was the problem.

I understood, the bit 'bout no one listening. I understood that bit, because no one'd listened to me either. No one understood why I couldn't eat the food that they said I needed to eat to get better.

'It's not that simple,' I'd said.

'It is, just eat,' the doctor'd said.

Six weeks later, Saturday the nineteenth of March, Sarah told me that she was itching to fly again. She told me while she was eating her tea, said how there wasn't enough height for take-off, not anywhere on our ward. She'd tried from the cistern, but ended up banging her head on the cubicle door; she'd been concussed when the nurse'd found her.

That day, Sarah said that she needed to get out, that she'd heard, 'bout a bridge 'bout half a mile away, that it'd be her highest challenge yet. She was itching, she said, really itching. She told me that she needed to spread her wings and fly, that being cooped up was driving her mad, that flying was what she was born to do.

'Will you cover for me? Just tell them I'm in the loo. Say I've got the splats,' Sarah said and we both laughed.

Turns out no one asked me where Sarah was, I don't even think they noticed that she'd gone, not until someone phoned. Then holy hell broke out on the ward, with nurses running around, patients being counted, lights going on in the middle of the night. Some of the inmates screamed, others sang Christmas carols; a change in routine brought out the worst in them.

I needed to find Sarah, because she'd know what was going on, she'd been cooped up on the ward for months, she'd know what to do.

I walked the ward, past the part-closed curtains, past the beds, past the other freaks, counted them, one two three four five six seven.

And then I came to Sarah's bed.

I found a nurse there, she was packing up Sarah's things into a Walkers Crisps cardboard box.

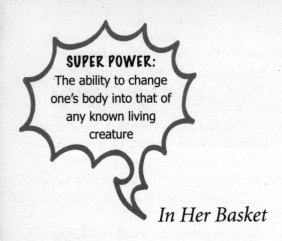

SUPER POWER:
The ability to change
one's body into that of
any known living
creature

In Her Basket

This is what I do:

First, I take off my clothes, leave them hidden in the field behind the bus stop. Now I vault her wall and I land in her back garden. I shrink myself down – turn myself into a cat – the same colour as hers (it's all in the detail) – and I squeeze through her door and into her kitchen. I pad over to the basket and curl up there.

I allow myself a happy meow. She'll be awake soon.

All I have to do is wait.

SUPER POWER:
The ability to amplify
memories

Fifty Per Cent

One

The love story ended on the beach. You know, I thought we were so happy, so together, so in-tune. I thought we were linked. But you did it again, that thing. And right then, right there at the beach, I realised.

You'd done it at dinner the night before. I was telling you my plans, suggesting a future for us, and you, you pulled away, you went somewhere else. Your eyes were not on me. I don't think you heard my words. I think you were looking for another future, one just for you. You were looking out of the window.

And, now I think about it, you'd been doing it for years. You were always late. Even on that first date I read the menu twenty-two times before you arrived. You didn't even look flustered. I don't think you'd rushed. Twenty-two times, Emma. I counted. I remember.

You were always pulling away.

It didn't matter where we were, we could be anywhere, you were always looking the other way, always moving away from me.

Your course at the university, your placement, your friends. None of that was for me. I was unwelcome.

It hit me on the beach.

I was talking. Do you remember what I said? I doubt it.

Emma, I was talking about the house that you said you liked. I was explaining how we *could* afford it. I'd done the sums. I had stopped to explain it all to you.

And you kept walking. I was no longer talking to you, I was no longer looking at your face. I couldn't see your eyes, your mouth, your fringe. I was left looking at your back, at your shoulders, at your ponytail. I was left looking at the shapes the soles of your feet made in the sand. I was left watching you walking away from us.

And I knew I couldn't stop you. I knew I couldn't follow. I knew I needed to let you go.

That's why I turned. That's why I went back to the car.

That's why I went home.

Two

Our love story ended on the beach.

We were walking along the sand. You were talking about that house, the one I'd needled you to view, the one I'd said we needed, the one I'd said I couldn't live without. You'd laughed, kissed my forehead, called me a drama queen. This walk was your way, a romantic gesture, you'd wanted to tell me how you'd figured out the sums, how we could afford that house. And I didn't even reply to you, I didn't nod or even smile.

Jamie, I'd wanted to tell you a week ago, I'd wanted to tell you at dinner last night. And then it hit me, right when you were talking about rising interest rates and first-time buyer incentives, right then I realised that if I didn't say my words out loud then my head would explode into a million squidgy pieces.

'I'm pregnant but I shouldn't be,' I whispered. I kept on walking, kept my eyes fixed on the pier, too scared to even look your way. I knew that if I saw even a flicker of joy, then I'd shatter into smith-

ereens. The wet sand tickled my toes and on any other day I'd have
made you take off your trainers and raced you into the sea. On any
other day I'd have been telling you just how alive I felt, that I loved
you, that having our baby growing inside of me made me feel
normal for the first time in my life.

'I wanted to tell you yesterday,' I whispered. I wanted to tell you
what the doctors had said. 'I wanted to say, "My heart doesn't work
properly", I wanted to say, "50 per cent". I wanted to tell you that I'm
not ready to take the risk.

'I can't have this baby.' The words rushed out.

I kept walking. I stretched out my arm to where I thought you'd be. My fingers strained to touch you. I hoped that you'd fold your hand into mine. Just for that moment, I hoped that you'd love me enough not to mind that I was faulty.

I stood still.

I buried my toes into the wet sand to stop me moving further away from you.

I turned, but you weren't there.

Invisible

If I stay totally still,
if I stand right tall,
with me back against the school wall,
close to the science room's window,
with me feet together,
pointing straight,
aiming forward,
if I make me hands into tight fists,
make me arms dead straight,
if I push me arms into me sides,
if I squeeze me thighs,
stop me wee,
if me belly doesn't shake,
if me boobs don't wobble,
if I close me eyes tight,
so tight that it makes me whole face scrunch,
if I push me lips into me mouth,
if I make me teeth bite me lips together,
if I hardly breathe,
if I don't say a word.
Then,
I'll magic meself invisible,
and them lasses will leave me alone.

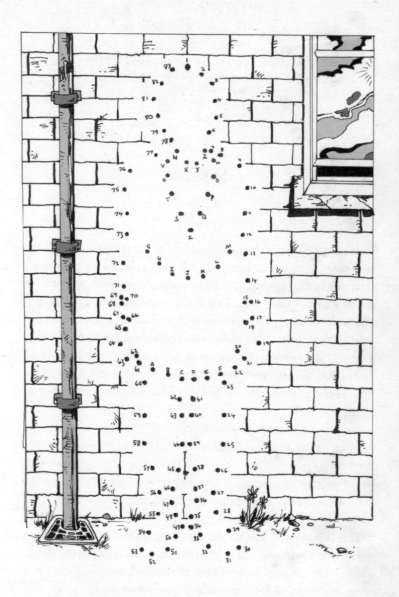

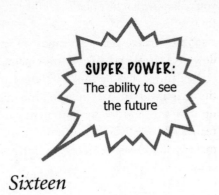

SUPER POWER:
The ability to see
the future

Sixteen

You stand in front of the pre-agreed shop window. Your hands are in the pockets of your best coat, the coat you've only previously worn for family birthday meals in restaurants, when you've been driven there by your dad. This is the first time you've worn this coat without your parents being with you and that makes you feel like an adult, but it also makes you feel exposed. You feel exactly what you are: sixteen, dressed up in tights and a pretty skirt – hair that's taken almost two hours to perfect (and it's still not right) – cold, in the middle of town, and nervous, waiting for this boy to arrive.

You have arranged to go to the cinema. You have no interest in the film, in fact you've no idea what the film's about; you're interested in this boy, this boy who's asked you to go to the cinema with him. And you're interested in knowing how it feels to be grown-up, to be doing this grown-up thing with this boy, even if it's just for one, cold evening.

This boy arrives. You see him striding towards you, and when you do you check yourself in the reflection you make in the shop's window. He's close now, so it's too late to back out – you can't run away; he's here, in his jeans and trainers and ironed shirt, and you're happy that he's made an effort, that this isn't just significant for you.

You exchange a Hi and then you walk together, side by side, down the street and towards the cinema. You are still cold.

You think that he looks different this evening. As you walk through town, you pass men and you think that, one day, he'll grow up into one, and for that moment you're reassured because you realise that, really, he's not quite there yet – like you – and that makes you feel safe or, at least, a little less nervous.

You each pay the man in the booth for your own ticket and then, purse in hand, you walk over to the confectionery kiosk. You've done this before so you're comfortable. This part isn't scary.

You say, 'Sweet or salty?' and he looks at you as though you've asked him the weirdest question in the world. At that moment you feel a mile away from him.

You flush, your cheeks tingling and red, and the muscles in your stomach tighten. You push your toes into the floor. This, the popcorn thing, is something you do with your family and you wonder if you're the only ones in the whole world who do it. You feel stupid and exposed and foolish. You think you look like a child, like when you tried on your mum's high heels when you were small, and, for a moment, you hate your family and their rituals. You're ashamed by them.

He says, 'You mean popcorn? I …' He pauses. 'I don't usually have it.'

'Okay,' you tell him, forcing a shaky smile. 'That's okay.'

'No,' he says, looking at you.

'What?' you reply, too quickly.

'If you want some, that's cool,' he says. 'We can have some if you want.'

'I'm not bothered,' you reply. And then, 'Do you want some?'

33

'Yes,' he says.

You say, 'But I thought you didn't want any.'

And so on.

Until you end up with two cartons of popcorn, one salty, one sweet, and with next to nothing left in your purse because he's only just got enough left for the bus home. And that's when you notice another difference between you, because your dad's picking you up; you just hope this boy won't see.

Ten minutes into the film and both of the cartons of popcorn are by your feet. And that's okay because you've ended up with the salty one and you don't like it much – this is back when you still had ice-cream on Sunday after dinner, with wafers and strawberry sauce, with hundreds and thousands and flakes.

The popcorn is by your feet because you're doing what, really, you came here to do. You're kissing, or rather he's kissing you and you're letting him and you're trying to make it seem like you know what you're doing, like you've done this before. You're almost wrestling with his tongue and his teeth feel strange and he tastes like nothing you've ever tasted. You're trembling a little, you're sweating, and you notice that you don't feel cold any more.

You like this feeling, you think. You feel grown up and *he's not stopping so you can't be bad*, and that feeling of achievement, of victory, is why you let him put his hand to your breasts – so small then – and it's why, a week later, you let him put his hand up your skirt and his fingers inside your knickers. That's when you let his fingers twist inside you for the first time. You feel like you're progressing. You feel like you're growing and that's good. It feels like you're ticking the right boxes.

Kiss Matt, with tongues.

Let Matt finger me.

Have a boyfriend.

Tick, tick, tick.

It hurts a little, his fingers inside you, but mostly it's okay. Mostly it's good, though you do worry that he can smell you and that it might put him off. You worry your mum will be able to smell you too, when you get back home; you hope that she doesn't because you've lied to her – you've told her that you were staying after school to talk to Mrs Wilson about your geography coursework, when really you'd planned to go to the park with Matt because you'd promised to give him a blow job.

All of this is to come.

Right now you're back in the cinema; before you've had a hand up your skirt, before you've had his cock in your mouth, before you've tasted his sperm or felt it on your hands inside his trousers. This is before he's learned to drive, before he's spent his money on a room at a Travelodge, before he's laid you on the bed and undressed you, before he's promised to stop if it hurts. This is before he's said 'I love you', and before you've said it back; before you've spent as much time with him as you possibly could, before you've fucked him in the back seat of his car, over and over, in the dimmest part of supermarket car parks. This is before he's met your parents and before you've been embarrassed when you met his dad (he had no mum) and before you've gone with his friends to the seaside for a week one summer, when he was so drunk he passed out on the floor of the room, still wearing the shirt he'd thrown up on. This is before you've woken up in the arms of his best friend, before you've realised that it could all be so different.

This is before all of that. This is back in the cinema. Before the noise and the smells of a house full of a child, before the nerves of the wedding, the dancing, the happy times, the itchy feeling of regret.

So, the popcorn cartons are by your feet. One has fallen on its side and the popcorn has spilled onto the floor and made it sticky. You notice this when the lights come back on, almost deafeningly bright, and you realise that you've seen nothing of the film, not one bit, and you notice that you're sticky too, like the floor, and sweaty and that your jaw aches. You have a brand new taste in your mouth, a taste that's lingering there, that's clinging to you, like it doesn't want to leave.

You're clumsy as you leave the cinema. You stumble along the corridor and move awkwardly down the stairs and onto the street outside. It's quiet and it's dark now and the skin on your face burns from the chill. There is no kiss goodnight from this boy, which you're happy about because, somehow, you think your dad might see and that would be the end of the world. You walk with him until you reach that shop's window, where you waited for him only a couple of hours earlier and you wait there, watching him walking away from you so he can catch his bus home. He doesn't look back, and that's okay too, because you still have his taste on your tongue and on your teeth; you have your memento.

And you stand by the window and you wait for your dad. It's cold now and so quiet and this, the street, the town, the shop window, the people walking past you, it is different, unfamiliar. It feels as though it's something you're not quite a part of and that scares you. You wish you were home, where it's safe so, shivering, you push your hands into the pockets of your best coat and you hope that your dad is not late.

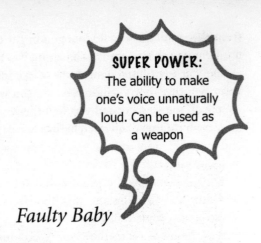

SUPER POWER:
The ability to make one's voice unnaturally loud. Can be used as a weapon

Faulty Baby

'You're imagining it,' she says. 'He's a tiny baby, listen to his little *ikkle* voice and his itsy *bitsy* gurgles.' She reaches over to baby Alfie and ruffles his wispy blond hair with her fingertips.

'You have no idea,' I say. 'Seriously Lu, he screams all day long. Incessant. He makes the windows quiver.'

'You're such a drama queen.' She laughs. 'Like this teeny *tiny* baby could ever be any trouble.' She speaks the words to baby Alfie in a sing-songy loopy voice. He gurgles and smiles.

'He hates me, seriously Lu, he hates me,' I say. 'He's faulty.'

Lu runs her fingertips down baby Alfie's face, making him turn instinctively to catch them in his mouth. She giggles.

'You're tired, that's all,' she says. 'It's normal for a newish mum to feel a bit off sorts.'

'Off sorts?' I say. 'Lu, I don't like him. Honestly. I don't like him.'

'I'd give anything to be you,' she says without taking her eyes off baby Alfie. 'You don't realise how lucky you are.'

I turn and I look at baby Alfie. I look at his smiling face and I listen to the cute tiny noises that he seems to make whenever others visit. It's like there are two of him, one good, one evil. I know that when Lu goes he'll start screaming again and he'll continue

38

screaming until his throat is sore, until my ears are fit to fall off, until the glass in the windows hangs on by a sliver of glue.

'Do you want him?' The words escape quickly, in my outside voice, loud and nippy.

'What?' she says, eyes turning to me, wide, sparkling.

'Have him,' I say. 'Seriously, have him. I'll get me a better one.'

SUPER POWER:
The possession of super-human amounts of strength

Dancing With Annie

The hardest thing is getting out of bed in the morning. Just like when I was a young man. When I was broken.

My fault, of course. I was showing off. Acting daft. Dancing on a wall.

'Dance with me,' I'd said. I'd told her, 'I'm good! I'm grand – watch!'

And up I'd gone, up onto the wall. Done my Fred Astaire for her. All for her. When she laughed I lit up inside, and I danced faster. I'd have done anything to see more of that.

'Will you dance with me now, Annie?' I shouted. 'Will you?'

She said yes. But I'd kept on. Couldn't stop and didn't want to. Faster and faster I went, her clapping. And she laughed harder and louder, clapping, tears on her cheeks, and then I fell.

I broke bones. It was a bad do.

And Annie, she visited. Promised me a real dance when I was up on my feet. When she touched my hand my pain went away. She was my angel.

I said to her, 'I'm looking forward to that dance.'

'So am I,' she said.

'If we dance well,' I asked her, 'do you think you might marry me?'

Turns out we did dance well and me and Annie, we wed. Me and her – husband and wife. Dancing together slow in the church hall. Friends watching, smiling, heads cocked. I'd said, 'You and me for ever eh, Annie?' and she'd said yes, pushed it into my my ear with warm breath.

And I kept my promise. We were together forever. For hers. Not mine though. And that's why getting up in a morning's so hard. Because there's no one to dance with. Or for.

SUPER POWER:
The ability to know and/or to control the feelings of others

Soup

Mike and Carol haven't noticed that I'm angry, but I am angry, really annoyed, because Ben's ordered the fishcakes and I wanted the fishcakes and when the waiter said, 'That was lucky, sir – that's the last one,' he should have said something. He should not have kept them for himself.

That waiter should be placing a plate of fishcakes in front of me. I should be smelling ginger and garlic and chilli and I should be pushing my fork under red salad leaves, but I'm not. I'm stuck with the soup.

'How's work?' Mike asks Ben and Ben says, 'It's going well.'

And it is. I allow him this. I let him feel big about himself because that way the fall will be more spectacular, more satisfying.

I say nothing, just nod when he says how busy he's been; he has. And I eat the fucking soup. The soup, I should add, is cold.

'Really pleased for you, mate,' Mike says. 'Sounds like you made the right decision.'

I wait until the waiter returns to stack plates on his arms.

'All this work's taken its toll though,' I say. 'Hasn't it, Ben?'

And I see the panic in his eyes. Ah yes. I know how this makes him feel, how much he worries, panics. It is a beautiful thing.

42

'Last night,' I say, calmly, 'Ben couldn't get it up. I think it's stress.'

I like the stunned silence. I drink it up, that and the awkwardness, like it's honey or sunshine or wine.

And then I say, 'Does anybody else fancy dessert?'

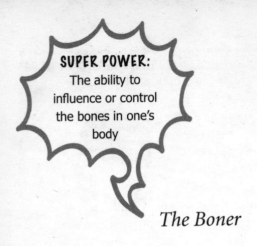

SUPER POWER:
The ability to influence or control the bones in one's body

The Boner

'Is there someone who needs a morning after pill?' the pharmacy assistant enquires a little too loudly.

She looks up. The pharmacy assistant hugs a black clipboard to his chest. His badge says *I'm Trevor*.

She stands.

'If you'd like to come into my office, I've a number of questions to ask you,' *I'm Trevor* says.

She follows him into the private room, an area just big enough for a plastic chair and a tall bar stool.

'Take a seat,' he says.

He hasn't meant it to be an order, but his nervousness has made his voice sound older and harsh. He tries to take a deep breath. He tries to calm down. He points at the plastic chair, his hand shakes. She sinks onto the seat, *I'm Trevor* perches on the tall bar stool.

'You need a morning after pill?'

His eyes focus on her mud-clad heels and he sees the trail of dried misshapen mud that has followed her into his office. He'll have to clean that up later. Then he looks at her shin, and then onto the hem of her pencil skirt. *I'm Trevor* feels his penis stirring. He covers his crotch with his black clipboard.

'Yes.'

'Have you had sex?' *I'm Trevor* reads the questions and tries not to imagine having sex with the lady in front of him.

'Yes.'

'Was it recent?' *I'm Trevor* enjoys his job.

'Yes.'

'Within the last twenty-four hours?'

'Yes.'

'Did you use any contraception?'

'No.'

'Are you aware of the dangers of sexually transmitted diseases?'

'Yes.'

'Was he a regular or casual partner?'

I'm Trevor thinks that the interview is going swimmingly.

The lady does not. With that question she raises her eyes and looks up at him. She sees that his black clipboard is balancing on what looks like an erect penis and she thinks that she might have been a little bit sick in her mouth. She sees that *I'm Trevor*'s pencil is poised to tick.

'Are these questions really necessary?' she asks.

'Before I can let you buy the pill, I need to establish if it will be effective. When did you last take a morning after pill?' *I'm Trevor* cannot meet her eyes. His mind has started to wander. He is hoping that she will make him sit on the plastic chair. He is hoping that she will kneel down and sniff his crotch. *I'm Trevor* knows that his penis is dribbling and he smiles as he thinks about her tasting it.

'I never have,' she answers.

I'm Trevor has forgotten the question. He takes a moment, a moment too long, to find his place on the list.

'Are you fit and healthy? Do you suffer from any of these listed?'

With this *I'm Trevor* unclips a form and hands it to her to read and sign. He cannot pass the clipboard. It is covering his erection.

She believes that she is healthy, so she signs the bottom of the form.

45

'You do realise that this is not a reliable method of *contraception* and should not be used as a form of *contraception*. You need to find another kind of *contraception*.'

I'm Trevor hasn't wanted to sound quite as obnoxious.

'I'm not stupid, *Trevor*. I know the facts of life. I ended up shagging Tim from work in that back field, just past the car park. I reckon it won't happen again,' she says.

I'm Trevor cannot rise from the seat. His penis is about to burst. He wants more. He wants to explode on the lady in front of him, the lady who likes to have sex with strangers, without condoms, in fields, in mud, in heels.

She rises, she towers over him. *I'm Trevor* keeps his left hand on his balanced clipboard and he holds out his right palm. A white rectangular box is on it. She takes the pills and opens the door.

'Please pay the assistant before you leave,' *I'm Trevor*'s voice quivers.

I'm Trevor removes the clipboard and closes his office door. He unzips his trousers and relieves himself into his boxer shorts. *I'm Trevor* loves his job.

SUPER POWER:
The ability to change
a person's size

Hello

You made me feel scared for the first time in my life. I mean, really scared.

I walked in there a man: with a house, a driving licence, a career – I even had a cat. And I was happy. I walked in there relaxed. I paused by the coat hooks when I saw you and, for long, splendid seconds, I simply watched.

And then you looked at me.

I think you had super powers in your eyes because you stripped everything away. Years of growth were lost in one glance. In a moment, because of your eyes, I was twelve years old again. No career, no car, no cat. I was back to having acne, back to having greasy hair.

I was nervous and I was scared. So scared. I knew what I could lose, you see, and I knew what I needed to do.

I needed to tell you that in that glance, in that instant, I'd fallen in love.

And that's why, even though I felt so small, that's why I said, 'Hello.'

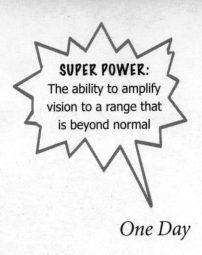

SUPER POWER:
The ability to amplify vision to a range that is beyond normal

One Day

That Woman collected plates, vases and trinkets. They were always blue and white. She'd spend her days searching in charity shops. She'd ogle, she'd gawk, she'd pursue. She'd squeal at the sight of a treasure that she was certain would be of value one day.

That Woman would cradle her find close to her china heart, making it feel a warmth of importance. Then in her antique home she'd seek out its value in her out-of-date-book, before carefully placing it in among her clutter.

That Woman would telephone her devoted daughter and then her faithful son. She'd relate precise accounts of her conquest, of how she had stalked and pounced to acquire her grail. She'd describe her find as money, as a promise of wealth that would bring eternal happiness one day.

But then That Woman died. And her devoted daughter and her faithful son waited a whole week before asking a man with a van to empty out That Woman's clutter. Her treasure was chipped and splintered, her grail was tossed into the man's heavy-duty rubbish bags.

'Nowt but crap, waste of me friggin' time,' said the man, a phone to his ear, before he rushed off to his next job.

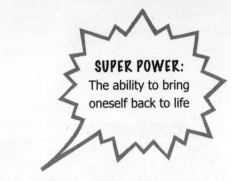

SUPER POWER:
The ability to bring
oneself back to life

Zombie Bangers

… so Lisa-Marie says to me – over the noise of that pink hairdryer of hers – she says, 'BZW on BZW'. Course that makes no sense to me, so I says to her, into the mirror – 'cause I'm like sitting down facing the mirror – so I says to her, '*B.Z.W.?*' Then she only goes and switches off that hairdryer, that pink one she uses for us special ladies, and then she's like talking from behind me, but like *to* me, but into the mirror.

… so she says to me: 'Big Zombie Women,' then she laughs; then she says that she's had a go on that resurrection.com. She says that she had a go 'cause she saw it on the telly and she says that she had no luck 'cause them blokes that goes on resurrection.com want nowt but fully decayed lasses.

… so Lisa-Marie says that her new zombie mate Pam told her 'bout the BZW inter-web-thingie. She says that it's like specially for big zombie lasses like her. I mean I don't think I've ever heard owt like that in me life. Anyways that Lisa-Marie says how she's a big lass, like I can't see that with me own eyes, like I'm not already thinking that it's a bugger she didn't get to rise again with a different body. Then she like jiggles her shoulders up and down and makes her massive knockers wiggle 'bout like puppies.

… so I says to her, 'You're fibbing.' I says, 'You've never gone and given the inter-web-thingie all your privates,' and she says to me that she has! I mean she says it like there's nowt wrong with saying it. She says that she's got herself a lush profile and she's only gone and told like the whole world her age and her eye colour and that she's a zombie and what she's looking for. I'm like lost for me words, then she's like laughing 'cause I reckon she can see that I'm like lost for me words, then she's switching on that pink hairdryer of hers and giving me hair another blow.

… so I waits a bit and I lets her dry some more of me hair, then I says to her, 'But Lisa-Marie,' I says, 'aren't you married pet?' Lisa-Marie says to me that she was, before she died, but how her husband reckons she's still dead and buried, even though she's like undead now. So I nods me head – like that makes any sense at all – then she says that if her husband finds out that she came back from the dead then he'd have a proper fit. She says that she's heard he's shagging her sister, then she laughs, but everyone in the salon can hear 'cause she's switched off that pink hairdryer again.

… so, then she's like telling me how she's been really brainy and how on her profile she's only gone and put up a photo of her new dog instead of one of her, she says that she didn't want no folk from her old estate recognising her and like telling her husband. Then she says that loads of blokes winked at her and how she got something like forty messages in one day, then she laughs again and then she like flicks her pink hairdryer back on.

… so I says to her, 'Blokes winked at you' – like with me confused voice again – I mean it's like I can't hide that I'm shocked, like really shocked – I mean it's like she's talking foreign with all her zombie talk and inter-web-thingie winking. So Lisa-Marie says to me they wasn't real winks – course she's laughing again like I've said something funny – then she says that she's been getting *computer winks*. Like that makes no sense to me, she says that something like loads and loads of blokes has been winking at her through their computers, and I'm like nodding me head, but really I'm thinking that Lisa-Marie's like one coffin short of a funeral.

… so then she's like putting her pink hairdryer onto the ledge below the mirror. It's like right close to me cold cup of coffee, then she says that them blokes – the ones on BZW – she says that them blokes like big zombie women like her. Then she like grabs her plump tummy, then she like wobbles her fat bits up and down, I mean I can't help but giggle – I mean I really giggle – it's like her fat bits are funny.

… so I says to her, into the mirror, I like says: 'Did you wink back at them?' Then Lisa-Marie does like a silly laugh, then she like bends over, like she's squeezing them fat thighs together, like she needs a wee. Then she says that she's only gone and found herself a London man. So I says to her, 'You hasn't!' I reckons that I says it like a bit too loud 'cause that Joel, you know that one who wears them purple shoes – well he looks over from reception and he like gives us like the filthiest look in like the whole world!

... so Lisa-Marie says to me – like she stays bending down close to me ear – she says to me that her London man works up here one day a week, she says that he's got himself a wife back home, like that's okay 'cause that's what them sort do. She says he's thirty-eight and he's a zombie banger and she reckons that he's like drop dead gorgeous. I like laugh 'cause I mean I've nowt 'gainst Lisa-Marie but she ain't no looker, then she only goes and says that she shagged the pants off him the first time she met him.

... so I says to her, 'You've met him?' I mean I practically yelps the words out, 'cause I sees meself in the mirror and I sees that me mouth's like wide open, I mean I couldn't help but laugh at meself. I look a right state, I look shocked. Then I sees that Lisa-Marie's laughing at me into the mirror, like she's some sort of brilliant slappy-sticky clown with one hand on her belly and the other pointing at me.

... so Lisa-Marie says to me that she's making the most of her time living, 'cause she reckons she's another five weeks before she dies again. So I looks at her with me sad eyes and she laughs and says that she'll be back again and I don't even ask her how, I mean she's like some sort of criminal zombie masterpants. I mean, I don't think we can trust owt that comes out that dirty mouth of hers. But it's like she's not bothered what none of us lot thinks of her, and she's not bothered that she's a proper zombie, 'cause she like laughs real laughs like all the time, she like laughs and her tummy and her knockers wobble up and down.

... so I says to Lisa-Marie, 'Lisa-Marie,' I says, catching her eye in the mirror, 'you know, I reckons you're probably like the happiest zombie I've ever met.'

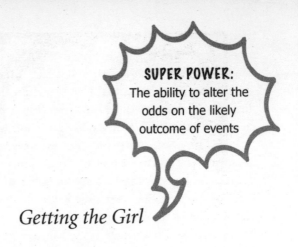

SUPER POWER:
The ability to alter the
odds on the likely
outcome of events

Getting the Girl

It's always about who gets the girl, isn't it? Especially at that age.

So. There are three guys all chasing one girl: Beautiful Emma. If this was America she'd be a prom queen and if this was a fairy tale then she'd be a princess. She is pale and beautiful and pure.

And who's interested?

There's Danny, the sweet one. Danny's written her a song.

There's Chris, the good-looking one. He's the guy who could have any girl in their year, pretty much.

And there's quiet Paul who knows her from maths.

And what's the plan?

It's a bit of a game to tell you the truth. It's like something you'd watch on the TV.

Three dates, one location: the bowling alley. And at the end of the evening, after the three dates with the three suitors, Beautiful Emma will choose who will take her to the party the following week. It's a big one. It's important. The guys have a one in three chance.

The game begins at seven.

By six all three are ready, prepared. They're pacing bedrooms, checking themselves in mirrors, applying aftershave, fixing their

hair. They're practising moves, lines, songs. They're rehearsing, going over their plans.

They all had plans all right, but only one worked.

Paul's. In fact, Paul's plan was so good that he's the only one who made it to the date.

He has Beautiful Emma on her own now, all to himself. He thumbs the length of cord in his pocket and contemplates the odds of getting some action tonight.

The odds, he knows, are in his favour.

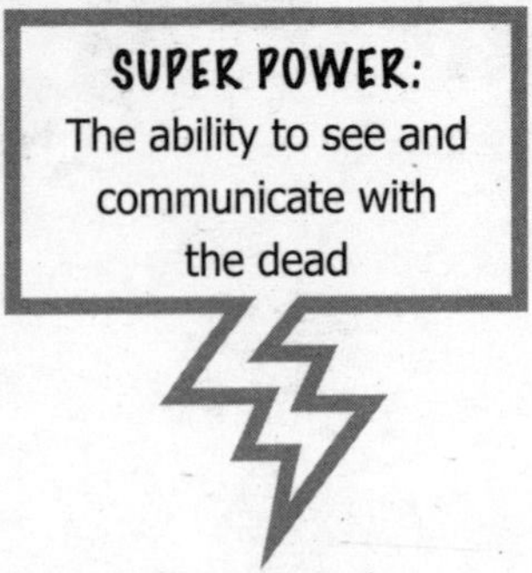

SUPER POWER:
The ability to see and
communicate with
the dead

They Are There to Listen

The medium turns to the mum, turns to the dad.

'Now, are you listening?' she asks.

'Yes,' they say.

'He wants to know ...' the medium continues.

'Yes,' says the mum.

'Yes,' says the dad.

'Why now?' asks the medium. 'He wants to know, why *now*?'

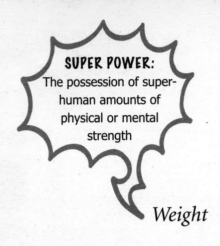

SUPER POWER:
The possession of super-human amounts of physical or mental strength

Weight

'WeCanSaveYou.com, Dione speaking, how can I help you?'

Dione sighed. Atlas frowned at her.

'Another wannabe jumper,' Dione whispered, hand over the mouthpiece. She twirled her right index finger at her temple.

Atlas tried to smile. She opened her compact mirror and peered at her reflection. 'Look at the state of my eyes,' she said. 'This job'll be the death of me.'

'Like you've got anything to worry about. You're flavour of the month, again,' Dione whispered, her hand still firm over the mouthpiece.

'It's all about communication,' Atlas replied. 'Make sure the caller really talks about their suicidal feelings, you have to truly listen. Remember what the manual says—'

'This job's a bunch of bollocks, if you ask me,' Dione interrupted, then laughed.

But Atlas didn't agree.

'Shit! I WAS listening, don't go, don't …' Dione shouted into the telephone. 'Oh bollocks, that's another one lost.' She marked a cross next to caller number eighteen. 'I'm crap at this job, I mean it's all so doom and friggin' gloom.'

'Doesn't it even bother you?' Atlas asked. 'That you've let another person slip away?'

'Get a grip pet! It's only a ruddy job,' Dione said.

'All those lost lives,' Atlas whispered. 'All those people who wanted you to listen.'

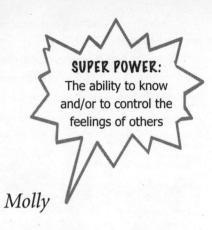

SUPER POWER:
The ability to know and/or to control the feelings of others

Molly

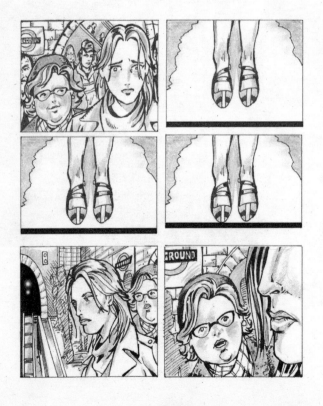

I've a daughter, you said.
She's my world, you said.
She's eighteen months old, you said.
Such a lovely age, I said.
She'll be walking, I said.
She'll be discovering new foods, I said.
She'll be developing her personality, I said.
Yes, you said.
All of that, you said.
I always wanted a daughter, I said.
Never happened, I said.
You're lucky, I said.
I smiled. You didn't smile.
Are you okay? I asked.
Not really, you said.
But we've just met, you said.
But you've one of those faces, you said.
But I shouldn't tell everyone I meet, you said.
It'd be wrong, you said.
To tell everyone that my baby is dying, you said.
That every day she lives is a blessing, you said.
That she's defying science, you said.
That she's flouting nature's rules, you said.
That one day soon she'll not wake up, you said.
She's all I've got, you said.
She's my world, you said.
You stopped talking.
The train pulled into the station.
You sighed. You stepped forward.
What's her name? I asked.
Molly, you said.
Molly, I said.
You smiled. I walked away.
And I knew what you were going to do.

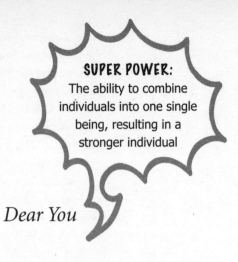

Dear You

Dear You,

You changed me when we met. You zapped me. You made me, me.

You see, before, I was fat. With you, I was an athlete.

Before, I had a job. With you, I had a career.

Before, I was ugly. With you, I was a lover. And I was a friend as well, and not lonely. I wasn't scared any more. I was alive.

I still think about us, you know. Sometimes. Sometimes I pretend that things are just as they were, but when I look in the mirror there's no athlete looking back. There's just me.

I long to be a lover again. I want to be a friend.

We were so much better as one, you know. As one, we worked.

Love,
    One Half of Us.

> **SUPER POWER:**
> The ability to know
> someone through
> physical contact

Control

This is what I want you to do, old man. I want you to meet me in the car park, near the back, where it's dark. I'll wait there for you, so you can finish your drink. It's okay.

First I want you to ask me what we're doing here. 'What's up?' you'll say.

And I'll tell you. I'll put my hand to your trousers and I'll say, 'I want you to fuck me,' because that's what I want you to do. Kiss me first. Kiss me strongly. I want to feel your beard against my face. I want its grey to scratch my skin, to make it red.

Then I want you to put your hands on me – shoulders, neck, cheek – wherever you want. You're in control. Put your old hands under my top, old man. Pinch my nipples with your fingers. My skin is smooth, and I want you to feel that. I want you to know that my body is hairless and skinny.

I want you to pull down my knickers. I'll kick them off, lose them to the dark and to the tarmac.

And I'll hold you, if that's what you want. Or tug you.

You are in control.

I want you to fuck me then. I want you to fuck me like you fucked girls when you were a young man, when you and Dad used to go out. Before Dad was Dad, when he was nothing but Mike. When he was just a man.

I don't want to enjoy you fucking me but I need to know how it feels. I need to know what you'd do, and how you'd do it.

After, when I'm looking for my knickers, while I'm scrambling over the tarmac, knees as raw as the skin on my face, the ghost of your cock inside me, I want you to go. I want you to leave me. I want you to leave me to feel what it's like to be closer to Dad.

And as you go, I want you to want to help me again.

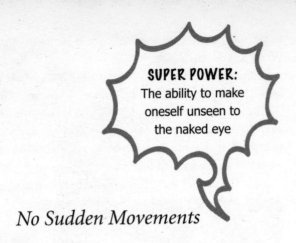

SUPER POWER:
The ability to make
oneself unseen to
the naked eye

No Sudden Movements

You will make no sudden movements. You will find a table in a corner and you will sit at it after you've, quietly, hung your coat on the back of a chair. You will drink something in small sips, lager or wine – not coffee because coffee smells and the steel spoon will tinkle against the cup. You need to be hushed. Quiet. Sshhh.

Then you'll pull out your book. Read it. Turn its pages carefully, keeping quiet, all the while remaining unnoticed.

Later, when it's time, you'll push your book into a coat pocket and stand. Do not scrape the chair over the floor. Do not return your glass to the bar. You will be quiet. Simply slip on your coat and leave.

No one will have seen you. You will have been invisible.

You will be free to follow her home.

SUPER POWER:
The ability to enter another's dreams

Dream Lover

One

He pushed himself into her dream with a pop. It was as though he'd stepped through a wall of honey, sweet and thin and soft.

And here he is. In her room, watching her sleep, her hair spread over the pillow like a crown or a blackened halo.

He touches her cheek to wake her. He's soft and gentle and as she rouses, as she pulls herself from the nothing of sleep, she frowns. She's still frowning when she sees him, and he understands, he knows how it feels to be pulled from a place so safe and comfortable.

He offers her his hand and she takes it, allows him to pull her to her feet, and then close to him, so their bodies are touching. In the dream it all feels real: the heat pushing through the nightdress and his shirt, the smells – of whisky and cigarettes, of make-up remover and cleanser, their hands touching – this could be real life. They could be awake.

'You came,' she says.

'Like I promised,' he replies. 'I found a way.' And then, 'What now?'

She looks to the floor for a second, dips her head and her gaze and then she looks up, looks at his face. 'Now,' she says, 'we go. There's somewhere I want to show you.'

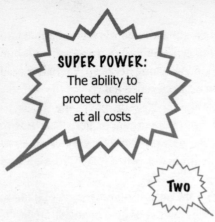

SUPER POWER:
The ability to
protect oneself
at all costs

TWO

I could hear the words coming out my mouth, but they weren't my fucking words.

I open my eyes.

'You came, like you promised? I want to show you something? What the fuck?' I say. 'Piss off, will you, you freakin' nutter,' I say. 'Stop entering my fucking dreams, will you.'

It's the same, every night. I fall asleep and that freak manages to pop himself into my dream. It's like my dreams are one of them boring black and white movies that my gran used to obsess about. I close my eyes, hoping for a good kip and then I'm seeing myself on a screen all floaty and sickly and puffy and pathetic.

I don't get it. I swear, I'm not into happily ever after and I'd certainly never be seen in a nightdress with some crazy wind machine making me look all blowy and weird. I mean, what's with the coy eyes? What's that all about? And if some crazy stalker bloke was watching me sleep and touching my face with his creepy freaky fingers, then I'm much more likely to wake up and smack him in the face. I mean, in my dreams, I'm practically jumping into his arms. What the fuck's that about?

But there's something, something that I just can't shake. Something that makes me pull my duvet up tighter and bawl. I mean, it's his smell, it's him. It's that familiar feeling that yanks at me, like I've known him, like I've needed him, that I'm terrified I'll lose him. Like him not being in my life is the worst thing. And every time I wake up and tell him to fuck off it's not because I want him to, not really. It's just easier. It's like seeing what happens next would somehow break me, it's like taking that extra step would make me realise everything I can't have.

And, if I'm being proper honest, each time he goes I'm left with my stomach bubbling and I want to throw up. Because he's not here. Because I've got to go another whole day without touching him. Because that freakin' nutter makes me feel something. Because, I know he's the one person in this fucked up world that could make me better.

SUPER POWER:
The ability to mask
one's true form

Once I Caught a Fish Alive

One

It started behind the bar. You watched it happen. You watched the water from the sink overflow onto my flip-flopped feet. I buckled, I crumbled to the floor. You watched as my foot flip-flapped into a scabby tail.

You said, 'Bloody hell! You're a mermaid.'

I was a bit sick in my own mouth and had to wait on the floor till my feet flicked back. You came and sat next to me. You bought me a drink and told me I was someone beautiful. Course, I couldn't talk back, but I could listen and nod and smile and blush.

Two

I nearly didn't go to your party, but then a taxi went past and I hailed it. I gave the driver that little slip of paper with your address on it and before I could change my mind I was on my way to your flat.

Three

You opened the door and threw your arms around me.

You said, 'I'm right pleased you made it.'

I brought a bottle of white wine. It had a screw top and was warm. You'd ran out of drinking glasses, so you poured me half a pint into a plastic measuring jug and showed me into the front room.

That's where John and Rosie and Penny and Stu were sitting. You introduced me to them all. John was strumming his guitar and Rosie was singing along. Her voice was gravel and her hair was blue. I sat on a cushion on the floor and you sat beside me. I sipped my wine from the plastic measuring jug and swayed in time with the music. You put your arm around me and I felt beautiful.

Four

And then the music stopped.

That's when John whispered something to Rosie and they both looked straight at me.

John said, 'You're the girl that can do that thing.'

I looked at you and you smiled.

Rosie said, 'That thing in water.' She stood up and came to sit down next to me.

Penny said, 'You're her.' She shuffled closer.

Rosie said, 'Quick, John, run the bath.'

I turned to you and I tried to speak but my words wouldn't make the sounds that your ears could hear. I used my hands, trying to tell you that I didn't want to go near water, that I needed not to go near water. I tried, but you weren't looking at my hands.

Five

That's when I felt John gripping under my arms. He started pulling me to my feet. Rosie snatched the plastic measuring jug and tossed it aside. I saw the wine dance across the room. Penny pulled off my flip-flops. You knelt up and started undoing my belt.

Rosie said, 'A freakin' mermaid.'

I shrieked as John dragged me to the running water, but you couldn't hear.

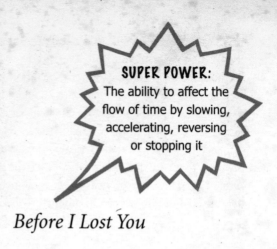

Before I Lost You

In a minute I'll be back in Liverpool. I'll be nineteen and drinking a pint of cider and black in The Ugly Swan. It'll be noisy. I'll be wearing a short shirt, there'll be no pointless stretch marks on my belly. I'll be happy; I'll have never felt loss.

In a minute I'll be smoking, liking the taste. I'll be taller, wearing ridiculously high heels, there'll be nothing sensible about them. I'll be holding my head up higher, I'll have perfectly curly hair. I'll have touchable breasts, a cleavage that is noticed. I'll have no lines on my forehead, there'll be no dark rings under my eyes. I'll be wearing White Musk perfume from the Body Shop and it'll not smell cheap.

In a minute some bloke will be trying to chat me up, he'll be saying that he's a drummer from a band that I recognise. I'll be impressed. He'll be saying that he'd like me to go to a party with him tomorrow; it'll be for his Aunty Rita, she'll be a traffic warden who'll have just received a CBE off the Queen of England.

In a minute I'll be in a taxi with him, too drunk, and we'll go to his crappy flat. I'll wonder where his drum kit is, why he's poor. I'll let him do whatever he wants to me. I'll think that I can make him love me. I'll let myself be twisted and turned into positions. I'll be performing.

In a minute I'll wake in his flat, he'll be embarrassed, in a hurry, he'll be needing to meet some bloke somewhere. Aunty Rita's party won't be mentioned and my breath will smell stale; he'll not ask for my phone number and he'll not check to make sure I've enough money for the taxi.

In a minute I'll be back in my bed. I'll be twenty, I'll be empty. I'll be back in my maternity trousers, they'll have an elastic waist.

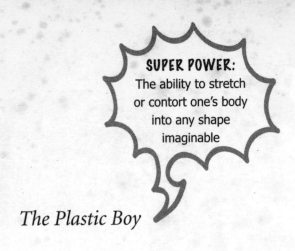

The Plastic Boy

This boy was different. This boy was made of plastic. He'd learned that he could squeeze into the tightest of places and that he could reach any point in his house from his room, easily.

At night, when everyone was asleep, he would pull open his window and stand at it, and look out over the town; see a thousand lonely, yellow lights.

And he would reach out then, stretch his arms as far as he was able to, and he'd reach out for his mother, for that hug. Mostly, all he felt was tarmac or pavement, or lawn or walls, rough against his fingers. Once, he felt the sand on the beach, cool from the water and the night. This boy wrote a message in the sand with a finger.

And this boy still stands at the window, the breeze in his hair, waiting for a reply.

Translated

'Dan il-bank bilfors imxarrab,' she says. **[This bench must be wet.]**

'Your fat arse must be wet, that bench is soaking,' he says, he smiles.

She laughs. He laughs.

'Nixtieq li kieku tista' titkellem bil-lingwa tiegħi,' she says. **[I wish you could speak my language.]**

'I understand you, bitch, you just don't realise,' he says, he smiles.

'Hilary,' she says pointing at herself.

'I fuckin' know you're Hilary, I mean I've been watching you, intercepting your post,' he says, he smiles.

'Skużi? Skużi?' Hilary says. **[Pardon? Pardon?]**

'Andrew,' he says pointing at himself.

Hilary nods. Andrew nods.

'Dan l-aħħar rajtek f'kull post li mort,' Hilary says. **[Recently I've seen you every place I've been.]**

'That's 'cause I'm watching you,' Andrew says, Andrew smiles.

'Donnu li d-destin irid li aħna nibqgħu flimkien,' Hilary says. **[It's like we're destined to be together.]**

'I want to carve my name into your flab,' Andrew says, Andrew smiles.

'Skużi? Skużi?' Hilary says. **[Pardon? Pardon?]**

Andrew laughs. Hilary laughs.

'Inħobb il-ħoss li tagħmel il-vuċi tiegħek,' Hilary says. **[I like the sounds that your voice makes.]**

'I like that you can't understand a motherfuckin' word I'm saying,' Andrew says, Andrew smiles.

'Inħobb il-ħoss tal-vuċi tiegħek, kompli tkellem,' Hilary says. **[I love the sound of your voice, keep talking.]**

'I'm going to kill you. I'm going to make you squeal like a fat pig,' Andrew says, Andrew smiles.

And Andrew laughs. And Hilary laughs.

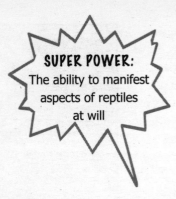

SUPER POWER:
The ability to manifest
aspects of reptiles
at will

The Girl Who Made People Glad

When I told Mum I didn't want to be Chameleon Girl no more, she
told me she wished I'd never been born. But I'd had enough of it.
Had enough of the changing colour, of flicking my tongue to the
ceiling, of making the boys glad. I'd had enough of being a star.

But then I went and met you.

You said, 'Nice tail.'

You had gentle eyes and floppy hair. I liked you. I didn't have the
words to tell you how you made my insides bubble. That's why I
performed those tricks, that's why I tongued around words. I
wanted to make you glad.

You said, 'Why you holding your breath?'

I'd been trying to become your favourite colour, blue, green,
pink, red. I'd wanted my skin to prickle out a new pattern just for
you. But nothing had happened, I'd stayed being me. I was peachy
with a tinge of blue. I was ugly. That's why I flicked my tongue up
to the ceiling that time.

You said, 'What's with the daft tongue?'

That's why I pulled my tongue back into my mouth and clasped
my palm across my lips.

You said, 'That's better.'

84

And that's why I was confused. I was normal, not blue, not red, not being a star. That's why I peeled off my clothes, down to my flaking skin. That's why I breathed in and I twirled. That's why I danced, I twisted, I coiled. I wanted you to be glad.

But you didn't move. You didn't strip off your clothes. You didn't say the words that all those other boys had spilled out and then sucked back in.

You said, 'You're a bit of a freak,' and then you smiled.

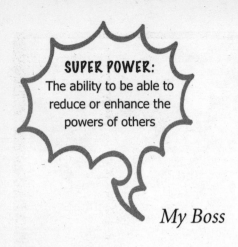

My Boss

It happens right in front of me. And I have to tell you, even though I've been hoping for this for weeks, it's kind of scary.

My boss, you see, he plays his wife. He has this way with him; it's so hard to tell him no, so hard to refuse him. He can make you believe anything he says, believe me.

I've been there, in his office, when he's had his wife on speaker-phone. I've heard her believe him when he's told her he has another evening meeting to attend, that there's no need to wait up for him, that he's really, really sorry. That he'll make it up to her.

And I've believed him when he's told me that he'll leave her. That I'm the one that he wants, the one that he needs, the one he thinks about. He's told me this before we've fucked and after we've fucked, and when we've been to dinner and in his car. I've done everything he's asked me to do, even when, sometimes, it's hurt.

But I've been getting itchy. Jealous too. So I sent his wife a present. Gave her evidence.

And here she is.

He's trying so hard to explain things, to tell her, but she doesn't believe him. She can't now. He looks so weak, so ordinary, now someone else has control.

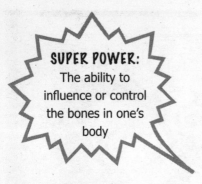

SUPER POWER:
The ability to
influence or control
the bones in one's
body

My Lover's Shoes Don't Fit Me (Any More)

My lover's shoes don't fit me. I've tried them on again. I'm moving through the house in them and their insoles are rough against my toes, rough against my heel.

My lover does not know I do this. She does not know how desperate I am for us to fit. I think I'm secretly hoping that my feet will have grown since last time.

They never do. There's always a gap. You could fit one of her cigarette packets between my foot and the heel now; I think I'm shrinking.

I clomp up the stairs in them, I'm up on my tiptoes so they don't fall off, and I drag them over the carpet and into the bedroom. I stand in front of the mirror. It's full-length, like mine. This is what I see:

I see myself reflected. The logo on my T-shirt's the wrong way round, garbled, unreadable.

My legs are like garden canes sticking up out of the shoes. They go straight up to my shorts. My legs are too thin, I think, too skinny for my shorts and my shorts are too baggy for my body. My feet are too small for the shoes and my smile's all wrong. The only thing that fits, I think, is the red around my eyes, and that's strange

because really this is a happy place; last night's dress hung over the chair behind me reminds me of that, of the good times, of the times when I can shut my eyes and feel that, just for a few moments, all is as it should be.

We're good together, me and my lover. I don't think I'd want anyone else.

But. I just wish there weren't so many gaps.

SUPER POWER:
The ability to change
one's size

Skinny Bitch

He was nice when I first met him, said he liked my skinny arse and my sad eyes. Everyone else had gone to bed, so just me and him sat talking together on the sofa in the patients' room. He was an artist, had long hair, had tattoos all over his hands, made them himself with needles and ink. I liked them, they were different, they were him. That night he kissed me on the lips, pushed his tongue in my mouth; I gave it a cheeky bite. He tasted of booze and ciggies, like a guitarist I'd once met at a gig, when I was a fatty.

I went to bed at 3 a.m., gave him a wink when I said night night. I liked him, even thought he might be the one to make me better.

Next morning I was waiting for my mam to call, waiting by the phone in the corridor. I saw him hugging a fat blonde lass, but not the three kids. He looked straight at me, his eyes warning me to keep my mouth shut. I did. I watched her giving him a bottle from her handbag, I watched him swigging it, I watched them buzzing themselves off the ward. He was wearing his slippers, I knew he'd be back.

When I saw him in the patients' room later I spoke to him. 'Nice kids,' I said.

'Not mine,' he said, his eyes looking at his hands, not at me.

'She your girlfriend?' I asked, moving closer to him. I wanted to see his eyes, wanted them on me.

'One of them,' he said. He turned to look at me then, ran his fingers down my cheek and over my lips. I stepped back a little, but not too much. It was a kind of surprise but I liked it. 'Told her 'bout you,' he said, his eyes finally on me. 'She's gonna kick your head in. One cup of orange juice and you're anyone's.'

I slapped his hand away. 'But, you kissed me,' I said.

He laughed, then winked.

'Fuck off,' I said, and I walked towards the door.

'You skinny bitch,' he whispered.

'Thanks,' I whispered back.

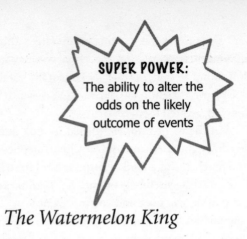

The Watermelon King

They have met at Għajn Tuffieħa Bay. They have three parasols, nine deckchairs and a coolbox that is blue. He sits on the coolbox, knife in his right hand, watermelon cracked open and balancing on his thighs. He hands one half of the watermelon to his wife. The water leaks from it and onto the back of his hand. He licks his lips.

His wife is in a deckchair, her legs out from the shade, her toes playing in the sand. She bakes in the afternoon sunshine. She takes the watermelon half, the flesh is a deep, a vibrant red. She smiles back at her husband. She is full of pride.

'Another good one,' she says.

'Every single time,' she says.

'You have the gift, my Mario,' she says.

Mario laughs, he likes the praise. He likes that he has the gift.

'She prefers to buy her watermelons from the mobile vendor parked near St Dominic's Church, in Rabat,' he says to the others.

'They are not always good,' he says.

'My favourite parks near the primary school in Birkirkara every Monday and Thursday,' he tells the others.

'You should go see him,' he says

'Tell him Mario sent you,' he says.

His sister laughs, Mario glares at her but it makes her laugh even more.

'Size matters,' he says to his wife.

'Bigger is better,' he says to the others.

His sister laughs again.

'Shush Maria,' his wife says.

'Show him some respect,' his mother says.

Mario smiles, his sister scowls.

'The trick is to tap on them with the palm of your hand,' he says to the others.

'If it echoes it's good,' he says.

'If the sound it makes is dull, it's usually bad,' he says.

'It's my method,' he says.

'Passed on from my father,' he says.

'And from his father before him,' he says.

His mother releases a sob and reaches into her pocket for her lace handkerchief.

'God rest their souls,' they all say together.

'The method works,' Mario says to the others.

'I never pick a bad one,' he says.

He cuts a slice of the watermelon, the others watch. He lifts the red flesh to his open mouth and bites. The sweet water dribbles from the side of his mouth and down to his chin.

'It tastes good,' he says to the others.

'Kemm hi tajba din id-dulliegħa,' he says. 'This water melon is very good.'

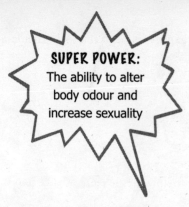

SUPER POWER:
The ability to alter
body odour and
increase sexuality

Dolly's Magic Sweater

Dolly and me shared a house. We weren't students.

That afternoon Dolly came in me bedroom holding out a present wrapped in the local free newspaper and tied up with one of the green laces from her Converse high tops. Dolly was all beaming and I couldn't help but chuckle.

'Happy Birthday to you, happy birthday to you,' she sang.

She came and sat down next to me on me bed.

'For you,' she said, passing me the present.

Me hands were shaking as I unwrapped it.

'A new sweater,' I said, offering back her laces.

'Woman in the shop said it was magic. It's made from that new-fangled fabric, makes your belly look three inches smaller without even breathing in,' she said.

'It looks expensive,' I said.

'Twenty-seven quid,' Dolly told me.

I stroked me new V-neck sweater.

'It's hand wash only and a bit puffy pink,' Dolly said.

'It's perfect,' I told her.

'It suits your eyes,' said Dolly.

I smiled.

'Try it on,' Dolly said, clapping her hands together.

So I stripped off me Star Wars tee and pulled on me new sweater as fast as I could. Dolly was watching all the time. I was breathing in.

The fancy fabric felt soft next to me belly.

Dolly leaned in closer. 'Lift up your arm, let me smell your pit,' she said.

I raised me arm into the air and Dolly leaned in, pushing her nose against me. It tickled. Dolly sniffed and giggled. I felt me cheeks turning red.

'You smell like carrots.' Her words were muffled. Her nose was still in me armpit.

I smiled. I held me breath some more. She was so close to me. I wanted to touch her shiny hair.

'That smell doesn't half make me want to shag you,' she said.

'You, wh-what?' I stuttered, the mixture of breath holding and shock making me spit.

Dolly moved her mouth proper close to me face. I could feel her breath dancing on me neck. Me nipples were rising.

'I can't help myself,' Dolly said. 'It's that jumper, it's like enchanted or something.'

That's when I felt her fingers undoing me pants.

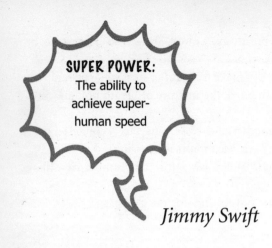

SUPER POWER:
The ability to achieve super-human speed

Jimmy Swift

They come once a year. When I was a boy it was like a second Christmas with presents and food, with laughter and noise. Only this gathering's in the heat of summer. It's always the summer when they come, when they invade our living room and cloud the air with their stories.

They've always had stories. The Bearded Lady would tell us of her kissing booth, and Mr Strong would tell us all what he'd lifted, how the crowd had screamed when he raised the pyramid of mammoths. Medusa came too, and she'd tell us of her beauty parlour, of how she could do things for anyone, even the ugliest, even the burned.

And then, at the end, as the finale, we'd hear about Jimmy Swift, about the fastest man in the south. He was the star attraction – he was what people paid to see. His act was a spectacular.

We were told how, first, the town would offer their naughtiest child.

Then, the cloth would be lifted from the cage and the crowd would gasp, they'd squeal and they'd cheer, when they could see the pacing, the snorting, the hungry Minotaur, as tall as trees and as

strong as the sea. A beast so rare, and so dangerous, that to be in the same room as it would send them into a gleeful panic.

That's when Jimmy Swift appeared and led the child to the centre of the ring, to the cage. The audience were encouraged to clap and the child was forced to watch as Jimmy stepped into the cage, into the beast's lair. Inside, Jimmy tormented the beast. He was so fast! He ran rings around it, prodded it, goaded it, whipped it. He made the beast angry. He made the beast furious. And when the beast was angry, when it was furious, when the sweat steamed from its shoulders and its mouth dripped hungrily, then it was time.

The gates were pulled open and the child was shoved inside.

The audience clapped harder, cheered louder. And the beast opened its mouth.

Of course, it was a trick. There were mirrors and there was a trap door and there was an effigy filled with the meat of stray dogs. So while the beast feasted, the child was safe, below the big top. The crowd and the beast had what they craved, the circus had another recruit and Jimmy was able to leave the cage and take his applause. Everyone was happy.

It only went wrong once. Once, is all it takes.

The crowd assumed it was part of the act and they screamed in delight and they clapped and they cheered as Jimmy's flesh was torn from him, as his bones were snapped.

And every year they come here to remember Jimmy Swift. They come here to toast him, to remind us of the good times, to remind us that Jimmy Swift was the fastest man in the south. That he was a good man. And they come to tell me about my dad.

Damaged

THOSE BEST FRIENDS GOT TO DRAW ALL MORNING.

THOSE BEST FRIENDS HAD SPORT EVERY AFTERNOON.

TERM WAS ENDING AND WITH EXPLODING
WORDS THEY TALKED OF SUMMER, OF
FREEDOM, OF BEING BEST FRIENDS FOREVER.

BUT THEN THE WEATHER BEGAN TO TURN. A STICKY CLIMATE THREATENED STORM.

LATER, A LOCAL PAPER RAN A HEADLINE
ABOUT AN ELEVEN YEAR OLD GIRL.

TOLD OF HOW EIGHT BEST FRIENDS.
SIX BOYS, TWO GIRLS STALKED THAT
ELEVEN YEAR OLD GIRL.

THEY HOUNDED HER.

THEY STRETCHED THEMSELVES INTO HER.

THE NEWSPAPER ARTICLE TOLD HOW THOSE BEST
FRIENDS LEFT THAT ELEVEN YEAR OLD GIRL ALONE.
DAMAGED.

SUPER POWER:
The ability to suck
love from people

My Dad's Boyfriend

That night my dad's boyfriend called him Freckles. His boyfriend said, 'You want a brew, Freckles?' And then the boyfriend laughed. I laughed too and the boyfriend gave me a cheeky wink. His eyes sparkled. My dad didn't laugh. My dad kept his mouth in a straight line. My dad's freckles shivered. He stared at the boyfriend until the boyfriend felt silly and left the room to make a brew.

The next sleep was when my dad croaked. Doctor said my dad had a wonky heart and that it was practically a miracle that I'd even been made. The doctor said that I wasn't to be too sad 'cause my dad's croaking would've almost definitely been fast and easy.

A few sleeps later and my dad was shifted to the graveyard, the one that's just over the back fence. That night I could see the gravestone from my dad's bedroom window. That night I shouted my dad updates of what was happening in *Coronation Street*. My dad used to love Ken Barlow's bottom. That night I knew that my dad'd never talk back but I still wished that I could go round to his plot and have a brew and watch the telly with him.

That night, when I was in my dad's bed, the boyfriend said that my shouting at dead folk was creepy and he didn't want my sex when my dad's curtains were open. I laughed at him, said he was a div, then I went down to his willy and kissed it.

SUPER POWER:
The ability to travel
through time

Betty

He travels most when they argue. So, instead of seeing Betty's face wrinkled and curled into a frown, he goes back to a time when her skin was smooth and lineless. He goes back to a time when he can see her when she's thin, when her ankles aren't swollen, when her hair is naturally black and when her teeth are her own.

He goes back to a time when her lips are smooth and painted and have hardly been kissed. He goes back to see her fingers when they're slim.

He goes back to when they fell in love – when love was excitement and laughter, touching and kisses and smiles, not sitting in different chairs in the same room watching the TV.

He goes back and he sees how obvious her beauty is, how she's utterly loveable.

And when he returns he sees that, really, not all that much has changed. He says he's sorry, that he simply forgot to put the bins out. He's sorry.

And he kisses her then, on her lips and they don't feel all that different, they don't feel old, they simply feel like Betty's. He thinks the same of her hand when he touches that.

When he follows her back into the living room, and they take their seats in front of the TV, he remembers that this is all he's ever wanted and he knows that life isn't perfect, but it's good.

SUPER POWER:
The ability to change
one's body into that of any
known living creature

I Want You to Ride Me Like a Pony

'Are you awake?' she asks.

'Mhurf,' he says.

'I want you to ride me, like I'm a pony,' she whispers, just loud enough for him to hear.

'You what?' He leans over and switches on the bedside lamp.

'I'm a pony.' She lifts up the duvet to reveal her naked breasts and a large pair of My Little Pony knickers.

He looks her up and down. 'Where'd you get them?'

'Off the market, three pairs for a fiver.'

'And you want me to ride you ...'

'Like I'm a pony,' she says.

'How the fuck am I supposed to do that?' he asks.

'I mean ...' she begins.

'It's not like you're even into any of them nature programmes on the telly.'

'I got you a whip.' She pulls out a little black whip from under her pillow and puts it on his belly.

'What the fuck!'

'It's called cosplay,' she explains. 'Steve Currie from the pub reckons that it'll spice things up no end.'

'You're wearing a pair of My Little Pony knickers, I mean it's hardly a costume, pet.'

She frowns. 'He reckons that if we get into it you can enter me for shows, win rosettes and stuff.'

'It's half one in the morning,' he says. 'Do I look like I want to be whipping your arse?'

She gets on all fours, sticking her My Little Pony knicker-clad bottom into the air and her head down to her pillow. 'Ride me, big boy,' she says, looking him straight in the eyes.

He laughs and the whip on his belly wobbles, then he leans over and switches the bedside lamp off.

'Oww,' she says. 'What the fuck was that?'

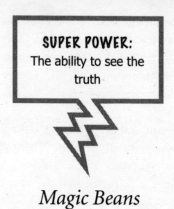

SUPER POWER:
The ability to see the
truth

Magic Beans

When Martin showed us those pills in the playground he told us that we could never talk about them, not after that day. We all took one. None of us were going to back out. But before we did Carl said, 'But Martin, what do they do?'

Martin closed his fingers around the palm full of pills. 'They're strong these,' he said. 'They're pure. Real pure.'

'But,' said Carl, 'pure *what* exactly? What do they do?'

'You take one of these,' said Martin, looking each of us in the eye for a moment, 'and you'll see everything as it is. You'll see the truth.' He smiled when he said that, and I did too.

'How long do they last?' asked Jessica, flicking her cigarette to the floor like she always did, putting it out with the sole of her ankle boot.

'Yeah, Martin,' I said. 'How long?'

'Not long,' he replied. 'But long enough. Plus – once you've seen the truth, you've seen it. Not like you'll forget now, is it?'

He was right.

So we took them. Each of us with our own pill washed down with a glug of raspberryade. And, after, we shared what we'd seen.

Martin had seen the world in different colours. He said it looked like everyone glowed and moved together. Like dancing, he said. Like everything just worked. Like the world was a really good place and that it made sense.

Jessica saw the future. She said that afterwards, once she'd seen it, she felt utterly happy because she knew how everything was going to turn out and that it was all going to turn out right. She said it even stopped her worrying about her exams.

I didn't get the chance to tell them what I saw, because the bell rang, ordering us to get to our lessons. I'm not sure what I'd have said if I'd have had the chance, because I saw nothing. Well, nothing but Jessica. And Jessica didn't see me. I suppose it's just as well she'll never know.

SUPER POWER:
The ability to
reverse time

Boy

This is how it ended.

It ended with me waiting till after nine, I knew the rules. I wheeled you along the corridor. You were in your plastic crib, I waddled in pink pyjamas, they stretched over my belly. My belly was large.

The phone rang, and rang. I expected it to go to answerphone, I knew that I couldn't leave a message but I liked to hear Nigel's voice. Nigel answered. He'd just dropped his girls at school, he'd been on a different call. Nigel's voice was loud, he was excited that I'd phoned.

'And?' Nigel asked.

'A boy,' I said.

'A boy!' Nigel said.

Nigel wanted me to describe you, he wanted me to say that you looked just like him. You didn't but I said that you did.

The payphone ate the money. I didn't say what I needed to say. The other new mums queued. I looked at them. Each smiled at me. I counted them, one, two, three. They listened.

'When can I meet him?' Nigel asked.

'I don't know,' I said.

'It'll be six weeks before we can do it,' Nigel said.

'It?' I asked.

'Fuck,' Nigel said. 'I can't wait to fuck you again.'

That was when I looked at you, my boy, when I saw you for the first time. You were beautiful, faultless, more than I deserved.

I hung up on Nigel.

Tears were already leaking from my eyes and snot already trickled out my nose. I turned away from the payphone. I knew what would happen next. I'd been there before.

The other new mums looked to their fluffy slippers and not at me. I shuffled past them, one, two, three.

'I'm going to send you back,' I whispered to you. I pushed your plastic crib back to the ward. 'You deserve better. It's time I made things different.'

I reached the hospital bed. The inside of my thighs ached. I stretched my hand to touch your forgiving skin.

'Goodbye,' I said to you.

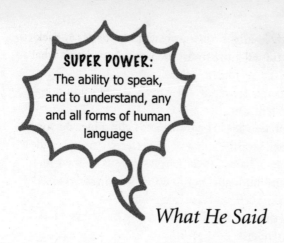

SUPER POWER:
The ability to speak, and to understand, any and all forms of human language

What He Said

She met him after his meeting. 'Je t'aime,' she said.

'Je t'aime,' he replied and he kissed her then.

'Je t'aime,' he told her after they'd made love, her wrapped in him, him wrapped up in the night.

'Je t'aime,' he told her in her car at the airport, as she dropped him off. 'Je t'adore.'

They strolled through the cool Berlin night in warm coats and woolly hats, hands together, his thumb stroking her skin. They found a café, sat outside.

'Ich liebe dich,' he said, between sips of coffee, their hands still touching, their lips the shapes of smiles.

In China, in the afternoon heat, sweat on their bodies like a second skin, he told her, 'Ngo oiy ney.'

She smiled first, then laughed.

'Perfect pronunciation,' she said, and she put her hand to his stomach, kissed his shoulder lightly, let her hair fall over his chest.

Home now. And with the kids in bed she hands him wine. 'Been in the fridge chilling,' she says.

He takes it, tells her, 'Thanks,' then, 'Cheers.' He sits on their sofa and she stands behind him, puts her hands to his shoulders, and rubs them.

'I've missed you,' she says and he tells her, 'I've missed you too.'

She rubs harder, tenderly.

'I love you,' she says and he says, 'I know.'

SUPER POWER:
The ability to hide
beauty

Wish You Were Here

One

We were squatting in his brother's flat in a complex that was being demolished. Each morning at 6 a.m. I'd hear the builders and wonder when they'd find us. He'd not be bothered. He liked the wakeup call. He'd tell me to make him coffee, while he shaved his chin over the sink in the kitchen. I'd make his stove-top espresso and he'd look at me and make comments about my face. 'Mein Gott, you're ugly,' he'd say. Then he'd leave me and go off to drink Berliner Weisse and smoke Gauloises with friends that I'd never meet.

That summer I'd leave the flat for thirteen minutes each day. I'd walk to Lidl, keeping my eyes on the flaws in the concrete. I'd fill a basket with sweetness and return to the flat. The rest of my day I'd spend thinking of you and bingeing in time with the bash and the boom of the falling walls.

He'd come back with the darkness, smelling of perfume yet still wanting sex.

But then, this day, today, I found a white envelope lying in the hallway downstairs. It was addressed to me, the sender was you.

You'd met me two years before. It was a night out for all the freshers from the department. I'd been giggly on tequila shots and I'd flirted with you even though you'd said you had a girlfriend. You'd kissed my cheek and given me a mischievous wink when you'd left. That was how we became friends. We'd meet each other every now, every then and each time you touched me I'd forget to breathe for a single moment. You liked me, I liked you, we once almost had sex.

Then this summer, this day, your words found their way to me. You wrote that you wanted for us to try to be together, that we would be good together, that we could have a chance at a happily ever after. You wrote that it was time. You wrote that I was beautiful, that you loved me, that you always had.

Today, this day, I moved my fingers over the loops of your writing in time with the bash and the boom of the falling walls.

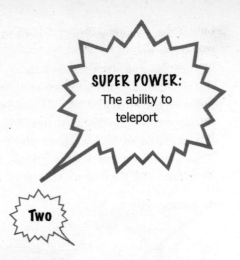

SUPER POWER:
The ability to
teleport

TWO

Lily,

I'm sorry I never told you about our connection. I think I was protecting you, and I liked the idea of keeping you safe. Maybe I was being selfish. I don't know.

That night in the club: freshers' week, London, Mitzi's Bar: that's when everything changed for me.

You see, I'd been able to take myself to different places for a long time, ever since I was small. I just had to concentrate hard on where I wanted to go and

ZAP!

I'd be there, almost. The thing was, while I was there, in those other places, I couldn't feel, I couldn't touch. I wasn't grounded, if that makes sense.

So, Mitzi's Bar. London. All those years ago. You, Lily – you were beautiful. I liked how you moved, liked how you had your hair. I wanted a closer look so I zapped myself over to you. You were flirting with me and you touched my arm and I felt it. I felt you. This had never happened before. That's why I kissed you – to make sure

126

(and really, my God, how could I not – you were beautiful!). And I wonder now: how did it feel to you? For me it was like electricity between lips and cheek.

When you left all I wanted was to find you again. Did you not think it was odd how we met all those times – how we bumped into each other at the most random of places, how it was never planned? It wasn't coincidence, Lily, it was me. I was in my flat, every time, in my bed or on my sofa, thinking about you so very hard so I could zap myself to where you were.

That's the real reason we didn't have sex that time. I'm sorry. But I wanted to actually be there, I wanted to be there in body. I wanted it to be right. It wasn't that I didn't want to sleep with you, or because I thought you were ugly, or any of those things you said. I wanted to be with you, properly. I should have told you this then.

I wish you hadn't left.

And Lily, I'm so sorry if I was wrong in doing what I did, but I couldn't help myself. I followed you. I looked out for you. But I was careful you didn't see. From my sofa or bed I watched. I saw you with Paul Greenwood. I saw that argument with your mother. You know, you weren't wrong to do what you did: it wouldn't have been right, you were too young.

I followed you to Germany too. I watched you hooking up with him. I've seen where you're living and how you're living and how he treats you and how you don't seem to smile any more, and it's wrong.

You deserve better.

So, now's the time for honesty. Lily, I know this is clichéd but it feels like you really do make me whole. I think you always have. And I think we should be together, I think we should try to make things work between us because I think that we're in love.

We can do this, if that's what you want. I can't go on, just watching. I want to be with you, properly. I think it's about time, Lily, don't you?

SUPER POWER:
The ability to
maintain beauty

Beauty

I was standing in the queue at the supermarket checkout when the woman behind me touched my arm and said, 'I'm sorry if this is a bit odd, but you remind me of someone beautiful.' The strangest thing was that I could tell she meant it.

'Thank you,' I said and I reached for the plastic divider and placed it on the conveyor belt. She watched my face the whole time. I could see her out of the corner of my eye and I could feel it too.

I turned to look at her and she smiled seriously, then she continued; 'Sorry. You must think I'm a bit weird.' She frowned a little then.

'It's fine,' I told her. It was a nice thing to hear. She placed a box of eggs on the conveyor.

'So,' I said, 'who do I remind you of?'

She smiled. 'Does it matter? Beauty's beauty.'

'Okay,' I said.

'I'm not mad, you know?' she said.

I told her I believed her, which I kind of did. There was something about her I liked, not that I could put my finger on it. She had good hair, I remember noticing that. And good legs. Nice eyes too.

'You look nice too,' I told her and she said, 'I wasn't fishing for compliments.'

She looked hurt so I apologised. I told her I meant it though.

She said nothing for a few moments, concentrated on pulling items from her basket and stacking them on the conveyor. There were vegetables (courgettes, bell peppers and a cauliflower) and a fresh fish.

'So,' she said.

'So?' I replied.

'So, you remind me of someone beautiful and you want to know who?'

I told her 'Yes,' but that, also, it was fine if she didn't want to say.

She smiled at me again, more relaxed now and said, 'Well, what do you think beauty looks like? When was the last time you saw something beautiful?'

'Kenya,' I said, almost immediately. 'A sunset. That was beautiful.'

'How?' she asked.

'It – it just was.'

She nodded firmly. 'Beauty's beauty,' she said.

After I'd paid I waited for her by the automatic doors. I wanted to continue our conversation and was hoping we could continue it over coffee – even in the supermarket's lousy café if I had to.

I waited for fifteen minutes before going back inside, and wandering over to the checkout.

And she was there, surrounded by men in suits and men in shirts. None of them looked happy.

It turns out her credit card wouldn't work. I offered to pay, I had the cash in my wallet and I handed it to her. She accepted graciously and with a firm smile.

As we left, as we slipped through the automatic doors, she said, 'See? That was a beautiful moment, wasn't it?'

'Yes, it was,' I told her and I asked her to join me for a drink.

'Beauty's beauty,' she told me again. 'Beautiful moments are rare. Best not to spoil them.'

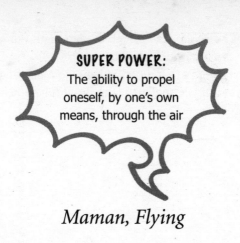

SUPER POWER:
The ability to propel
oneself, by one's own
means, through the air

Maman, Flying

When I was six Maman took me to her bedroom window to watch the migrating geese. They were pretty in the sky, over the fields, over the roofs.

In the summer, Maman took me to town. She took me up to the top of the Tour d'Eiffel, in the lift, and up to the balcony. Maman showed me how to feel the air, how to feel free. She showed me how to drink it. Said, '*This* is what life is.' 'Rienette,' she said, '*this* is life.'

Maman loved the sky. And I loved watching her love it. When she looked up she was dreaming, I think. And I think, sometimes, she'd have rather been a bird or a cloud.

On Maman's birthday, Papa took us out. We shopped, we ate lunch and I watched Maman watching the people walking by. They were so grounded, like dogs or sheep I thought, and I could tell that Maman was disappointed by them. We returned to the car. Climbed six floors to the top of the car park. I had a bag of Calisson. I offered one to Papa and he said no. Maman took one though. She kissed me on the forehead and then popped it into her mouth, crunched it behind her red lips.

Then she winked at me and she walked over to the edge. And I saw Maman fly.

Acknowledgements

THE AUTHORS WOULD LIKE TO THANK:

Scott Pack and Corinna Harrod at The Friday Project, whose many super powers include a superhuman vision for our book. Their support was wonderful too.

Our families, for their superhuman strength and patience.

Darren, for his supercool illustrations.

Fabri, who allowed us space in *that* cafe to put the stories in order.

And, you.

– *Nik Perring and Caroline Smailes*, the authors

THE ILLUSTRATOR WOULD LIKE TO THANK:

I have written two of these things before as a writer, but this is my first as an illustrator – not that I really class myself as an illustrator; it's just something I used to do in a past life before writing books and having kids got in the way. Thank you to my lovely iceberg and two little gems, but also to Caroline, primarily, for having me mind when she and Nik set out to create something entirely new and unique and diverse and in some cases just plain effed up (you'll see what I mean).

— *Darren Craske*, (whisper it) illustrator